Shoe Town

Written by Janet Stevens and Susan Stevens Crummel

Illustrated by Janet Stevens

SCHOLASTIC INC.

New York Toronto London Auckland Sydney
Mexico City New Delhi Hong Kong

There was a little mouse
who had a little shoe.

When her babies grew up,
she knew just what to do.

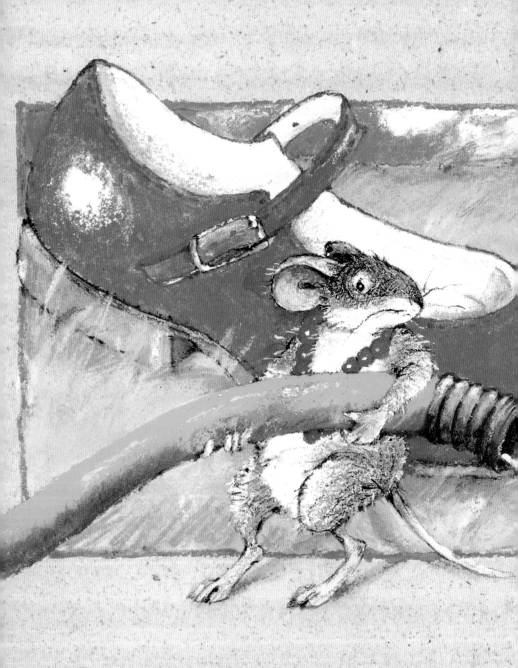

"I'll fill a hot bath,
then I'll take a long nap."

Just then at her shoe
came a *rap-tap-tap-tap*.

"We are Tortoise and Hare.
We just went for a run.

Can we stay here with you . . .
in your shoe? Oh, what fun!"

"My shoe is too little
for so many to share.

Look for a shoe, if you please.
It can go over there."

"Now I'll fill a hot bath,
then I'll take a long nap."

Just then at her shoe
came a *rap-tap-tap-tap*.

"I'm the Little Red Hen.
And I love making bread.

Is there room in your shoe
for one more?" she said.

"My shoe is too little
for so many to share.

Look for a shoe, if you please.
It can go over there."

"Now I'll fill a hot bath,
then I'll take a long nap."

Just then at her shoe
came a big *RAP-TAP-TAP!*

"I'll huff and I'll puff
and I'll blow your shoes down—

if you don't let me stay
in your little shoe town!"

"Don't huff and don't puff.
We'll be happy to share.

Look for a shoe, if you please.
It can go over there."

More and more friends came.
The little town grew.

And to think it began
with a mouse and her shoe!

ISBN 0-439-15327-1

12 11 10 9 8 7 6 5 4 3 2 1   0 1 2 3 4 5/0

Printed in the U.S.A.   *09*

First Scholastic printing, January 2000

The illustrations in this book were done in watercolor crayon, colored pencil, and watercolor with gesso on handmade paper.
The display type was set in Heatwave.
The text type was set in Minion.
Designed by Barry Age